Tudors and Stuarts

Fiona Patchett

Designed by Stephen Wright

Edited by Jane Chisholm

Consultants: Dr. Anne Millard and Janice Barter

The royal family tree

This family tree shows the dates that the Tudor and Stuart monarchs reigned.

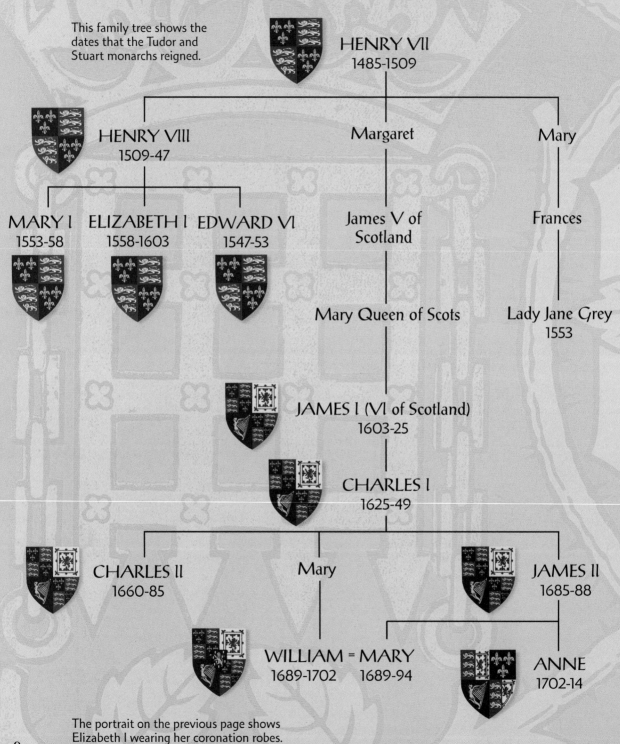

HENRY VII
1485-1509

HENRY VIII
1509-47

Margaret

Mary

MARY I
1553-58

ELIZABETH I
1558-1603

EDWARD VI
1547-53

James V of Scotland

Frances

Mary Queen of Scots

Lady Jane Grey
1553

JAMES I (VI of Scotland)
1603-25

CHARLES I
1625-49

CHARLES II
1660-85

Mary

JAMES II
1685-88

WILLIAM = MARY
1689-1702   1689-94

ANNE
1702-14

The portrait on the previous page shows Elizabeth I wearing her coronation robes.

Contents

Internet links

Look for the Internet links boxes throughout this book. They contain descriptions of websites where you can find out more about the Tudors and Stuarts. For links to these websites, go to **www.usborne-quicklinks.com** and type in the keywords 'tudors and stuarts'.

Many Tudor houses were built of wood and plaster. Little Moreton Hall in Cheshire is an especially grand example.

Who were the Tudors and Stuarts?

The Tudors and Stuarts were two royal families, or dynasties, who ruled parts of the British isles for 229 dramatic years - one of the most exciting periods in the country's history. It was a time of religious and political revolutions, sea travel and exploration and important scientific discoveries.

The Tudors ruled England, Wales and a tiny part of northern France (although they claimed rule over Ireland too). Scotland was a separate country then, ruled by the Stuarts, who often allied with France against England. But, in 1603, the Stuarts became kings of England too, and the two kingdoms were united.

Elizabeth I, the greatest of the Tudor monarchs, in a procession with her courtiers. She went on royal progresses, or journeys, twice a year to meet her subjects.

King and parliament

When the Tudors came to the throne, it was the king who made all the important decisions about war, taxes, religion and everything else. Parliament only met to give advice, pass laws and vote for taxes. It was up to the monarch to decide when to call or dismiss Parliament.

Religion and bloodshed

The British Isles were Roman Catholic, like the rest of Western Europe, and the Pope was an important political figure. But many people had started criticizing the Church and protesting against its corruption. All across Europe, religious differences led to bloody civil wars and persecution.

Art and culture

The Renaissance, a great revival of art and culture, affected all of Europe at this time. Inspired by a new fascination for the art, architecture and learning of ancient Greece and Rome, it led people to question the world around them and inspired artists, thinkers and scientists to come up with new ideas. The invention of the printing press in the 1450s meant that books could be produced quickly and cheaply for the first time, instead of being copied by hand. So more people could read.

Richard III, the last king before the Tudors

Before the Tudors

England had been ruled for over 300 years by a family called the Plantagenets. But, from 1455 to 1485, fighting broke out between two branches of the family: the Yorks and the Lancasters, who each claimed the throne. This was known as the 'Wars of the Roses'. In 1485, the Lancastrian heir, Henry Tudor, fought the Yorkist king, Richard III, at the Battle of Bosworth Field. Richard was killed and Henry was crowned Henry VII, the first king of the new Tudor dynasty.

The York emblem was a white rose and the Lancaster one was a red rose.

This family tree shows the York and Lancaster branches of the Plantagenet family.

EDWARD III
1327-77

Edward the Black Prince — John of Gaunt, Duke of Lancaster — Edmund, Duke of York — Others

RICHARD II 1377-99 — John Beaufort — HENRY IV 1399-1413 — Richard of Cambridge

John Beaufort — HENRY V 1413-22 — Richard, Duke of York

Edmund Tudor = Margaret Beaufort — HENRY VI 1422-61 — EDWARD IV 1461-83 — RICHARD III 1483-85

HENRY VII = Elizabeth of York — EDWARD V 1483 — Richard, Duke of York
1485-1509

Tudor
Lancaster
York
= married

Did you know? Richard III was the last English king to die in battle.

5

The first Tudor

Henry Tudor's victory at the Battle of Bosworth Field brought an end to the bloodshed and turmoil of the Wars of the Roses. As King Henry VII, he founded the Tudor dynasty, which promised the start of a new period of wealth and stability.

Families unite

To boost his claim to the throne, Henry united the York and Lancaster families by marrying Elizabeth of York. Later, he strengthened the status of his new dynasty by arranging suitable royal marriages for his children. His eldest son, Arthur, married a Spanish princess, Catherine of Aragon, and his eldest daughter, Margaret, married King James IV of Scotland.

The New World

Before Tudor times, most people didn't travel much and knew little about the rest of the world. But all this was about to change. Portuguese seafarers had recently discovered routes around Africa to India and China. In 1492, an Italian named Christopher Columbus discovered America. At first people called it the New World, because they hadn't even known it existed before. Henry VII was keen to encourage further exploration, so he sponsored John Cabot, an Italian navigator, to look for a quick route to the Far East. But, instead, he discovered Newfoundland, in North America. (You can see his route on pages 18-19.)

This portrait shows Henry VII and Elizabeth of York surrounded by York and Lancaster roses.

6

The Rose Window in York Minster commemorates the union of the York and Lancaster families.

Taking control

Henry increased his control over the nobles by taking more tax from them and stopping them from having their own armies. If they broke his laws, they were tried in a court, named the Star Chamber, and fined heavily. He increased his own wealth by confiscating the estates of his Yorkist enemies.

Internet links

For a link to a website where you can read about the ghosts that haunt the Tower, go to **www.usborne-quicklinks.com**

Plots and pretenders

Despite Henry's strong position, Yorkists still plotted to depose him. In 1487, they persuaded a boy named Lambert Simnel to pretend he was Richard III's nephew, Edward, Earl of Warwick, who they believed had a stronger claim than Henry did. But the real Warwick was a prisoner in the Tower of London, and Henry paraded him through the streets to prove it. Simnel was sent to work in the royal kitchens as punishment.

In 1491, a more serious threat came from Perkin Warbeck, who pretended to be Richard, Duke of York, Edward IV's youngest son. Warbeck claimed he had escaped from the Tower and fled abroad. He raised an army and invaded England. But he was defeated, imprisoned in the Tower and later executed.

Many enemies of the Tudor and Stuart monarchs were imprisoned in the Tower of London. This is the White Tower, the oldest part.

Did you know? Henry combined the white rose of York with the red rose of Lancaster to make a new emblem, the Tudor rose.

Henry VIII

When Henry VII died, he was succeeded by his 18-year-old son, Henry VIII. Fun-loving, handsome and popular, he was also arrogant and strong-willed. Henry married his brother's widow, Catherine of Aragon, and they had a daughter, Mary. But Catherine failed to produce the son he wanted, to ensure the survival of the Tudor dynasty.

This portrait by Hans Holbein, a German painter at the English court, shows Henry in fine clothes and jewels, to demonstrate his wealth and power.

Life at court

Henry loved huge banquets, sports, dancing and music. He played the lute, recorder and viol (an early violin) and composed his own music. Life at Henry's court was lively and exciting, but his extravagant lifestyle cost him much of the money his father had saved. He entrusted the day-to-day running of the country to his Chancellor, Cardinal Wolsey.

Internet links

For a link to a website where you can find out what Henry VIII was really like, go to **www.usborne-quicklinks.com**

Field of the Cloth of Gold

Wolsey hoped to establish peace with England's rival, France. So, in 1520, he organized a meeting between Henry and Francis I of France. Entertainment and sumptuous banquets were held in tents made of luxurious gold cloth. The meeting became famous as the 'Field of the Cloth of Gold'. But, soon after it, England and France were at war again.

This painting shows Henry VIII arriving on horseback, and wearing a golden cloak, at the Field of the Cloth of Gold in northern France.

The king's great matter

As Catherine got older, Henry worried she would never have a son. The problem became known in court as the 'king's great matter'. Henry fell in love with a courtier, Anne Boleyn, and wanted to marry her and divorce Catherine. But all divorces had to be agreed by the Pope, and the Pope would not agree to it. So, although Henry was a devout Catholic, he soon realized the only way to get a divorce was to break away from the Catholic Church in Rome.

A portrait of Anne Boleyn

The break with Rome

Henry's solution was to get Thomas Cranmer, Archbishop of Canterbury, to declare him Supreme Head of the Church in England. That way he could do what he liked without consulting the Pope. Henry then divorced Catherine and married Anne, but he was disappointed when she too gave birth to a daughter, Elizabeth, instead of a son. Eventually, he accused her of having affairs and had her executed for treason. By now Henry had already chosen his third wife, Jane Seymour.

Did you know? At her trial, Henry claimed Anne Boleyn was a witch.

Henry's new powers

In Europe, people known as Protestants were protesting about the corruption of the Church and demanding reform. Although Henry was not a Protestant, he broke all links with the Catholic Church in Rome and took full advantage of his powers as Supreme Head of the Church in England.

Closing the monasteries

Henry felt the English monasteries were too wealthy and immoral and decided to close them down. Thomas Cromwell, his new Chancellor, was put in charge of the project. The king took most of the proceeds for himself, but he also used some of it to build new schools and hospitals.

Fortress England

Since Henry had divorced Catherine and broken away from the Catholic Church, he began to worry that powerful Catholic rulers, such as the French and Catherine's family, the Spanish Habsburgs, would attack England. Making use of the stone from the abandoned monasteries, Henry built forts around the south coast to protect England from attack.

Fountains Abbey in Yorkshire was one of the many wealthy English monasteries that fell into ruin after being closed down.

The Royal Navy

Earlier English kings had borrowed cargo ships when there was a war on, but Henry built a navy of ships for the first time, just for war. He was especially proud of his flagship, the *Mary Rose*. In 1545, she set off to fight the French one more time. But the *Mary Rose* was so overloaded with cannons and men that she sank. Henry looked on, in horror, from the English coast.

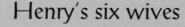

Henry's six wives

Henry's third wife, Jane Seymour, died giving birth to Edward, the son he had longed for. He then agreed to marry Anne of Cleves, a German princess, after seeing a flattering portrait. But he was horrified when they met, because he thought her ugly and nothing like her portrait. They married, but divorced soon after.

This is the portrait of Anne of Cleves that Henry saw, painted by Hans Holbein.

Internet links

The *Mary Rose* was raised from the sea bed in 1982. For a link to a website where you can take a virtual tour of the ship, go to **www.usborne-quicklinks.com**

At the age of 49, Henry married a young courtier named Catherine Howard. But that marriage was doomed as well. When he found out she was having affairs, he had her executed. In his final years, Henry grew fat and ill, and was cared for by his sixth wife, Catherine Parr. He died in 1547, after naming his three children as his successors, first Edward, then Mary, then Elizabeth.

Did you know? On his deathbed, Henry called out the name of Jane Seymour.

A child is king

Edward was only nine when he became Edward VI. His mother's brother, the Duke of Somerset, was appointed to rule for him until he was old enough to rule himself. But his reign was short and turbulent, and he never reached his sixteenth birthday.

Protestant reforms

With Somerset's support, Edward made changes to the English Church to bring it closer to the ideas of European Protestants. They preferred simple churches, so paintings, statues and stained glass windows were all smashed or removed. Church services were now held in English, instead of Latin, and the Archbishop of Canterbury, Thomas Cranmer, introduced an official English Prayer Book to be used by everyone.

This 15th century Flemish painting shows farmers shearing sheep.

Countryside in crisis

In Tudor times, most people lived in the country and made a living from growing crops and grazing their animals on common land. But, around this time, some landowners were enclosing huge areas of land with fences or hedges and farming sheep. Wool was now much more profitable than crops, but it meant that there was no longer enough land for poorer peasants to live on.

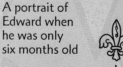

A portrait of Edward when he was only six months old

Internet links

For a link to a website where you can read about the short and tragic life of Lady Jane Grey, go to **www.usborne-quicklinks.com**

Country revolt

Many people were unhappy about these new enclosures and even tried to tear them down. In 1549, a man named Robert Kett led a huge rebellion in East Anglia. It was crushed by the Duke of Northumberland, who executed hundreds of peasants and seized power from the Duke of Somerset.

Plots and ambitions

Edward fell ill and it became clear he would not live long. His Catholic half-sister, Mary, was the next in line for the throne. But the ambitious Northumberland was concerned that, as a Protestant, he would lose power if Mary became queen. Edward also wanted a Protestant to succeed him, so he made his Protestant cousin, Lady Jane Grey, his heir instead. Northumberland plotted to marry Jane to his son, Lord Guildford Dudley.

The nine day queen

When Edward died in 1553, Jane was immediately declared queen. Mary was horrified when she heard the news. From her home in East Anglia, she gathered support, then marched to London. The Duke of Northumberland was forced to surrender and was executed for treason. Jane and her husband, Lord Dudley, were imprisoned in the Tower of London and later executed too. Jane had been queen for only nine days.

A 19th century painting of Lady Jane Grey's execution

Did you know? Lady Jane Grey was only 17 when she was executed.

A Tudor queen

When Mary was crowned queen, she was greeted with roars of applause from her enthusiastic subjects. But her five year reign was fraught with some of the worst epidemics and harvests that century, and she became very unpopular. She later won the nickname 'Bloody Mary' for burning hundreds of Protestants at the stake.

The Spanish connection

Mary was already 37 when she became queen, and she longed for a husband and children. The husband she chose was the Catholic Prince Philip of Spain. Mary hoped he would help her make the country Catholic again, but many people feared this might mean Spain would dominate England.

Philip before his marriage to Mary

Wyatt's rebellion

Hostility to the marriage grew so strong that in 1554 a landowner from Kent, Sir Thomas Wyatt, led a group of rebels to London to protest. Mary gave a rousing speech urging Londoners to help her, and with the army, they crushed the rebellion.

Calais is lost

Soon after marrying Mary, Philip became king of Spain and disastrously involved England in a Spanish war against France. In 1558, the French captured the port of Calais, in northern France, which had belonged to England for over 200 years. This had a devastating effect on Mary. "When I am dead, you will find Calais engraved on my heart," she told one of her attendants.

Catholic again

Mary turned back the clocks by making England Catholic again, completely undoing all the religious changes that had taken place under Henry VIII and Edward VI. She apologized to the Pope, made him head of the English Church and let all the Catholic priests out of prison. This time, the Protestant clergy were imprisoned instead. Over 300 Protestants, including women and children, were burned alive at the stake. Even Thomas Cranmer, the Archbishop of Canterbury, was put on trial and burned after he refused to deny his Protestant beliefs.

This portrait shows Mary aged 38.

This woodcut from John Foxe's *Book of Martyrs* (see below) shows Archbishop Cranmer being burned at the stake. This was the usual punishment for heresy (having the wrong religious beliefs).

Protestant martyrs

By the time Mary died in 1558, she was so unpopular that the day of her death was celebrated each year. A man named John Foxe compiled a *Book of Martyrs*, with accounts of Protestants who had been burned for their beliefs. A copy was put in every church to remind people of the horrors of Catholic rule.

Internet links

For a link to a website where you can find out about Mary's childhood, as well as her life as queen, go to **www.usborne-quicklinks.com**

Did you know? Mary twice believed she was pregnant, but both times it turned out she was suffering from an illness instead.

15

The golden age of Elizabeth

Elizabeth I, who succeeded her half-sister, Mary, was one of the most successful monarchs in European history. England prospered and became an important European power, and art and culture thrived. Elizabeth created a strong image for the monarchy and her reign is often described as a 'golden age'.

Movers and shakers

A skilled politician and diplomat, the queen was advised by a small group of politicians, known as the Privy Council, led by William Cecil, her Secretary and later her Lord Treasurer. Elizabeth and Cecil tried to save money by avoiding expensive wars overseas.

The Virgin Queen

Tall and slender, with curly red hair and pale skin, Elizabeth is sometimes called 'the Virgin Queen', because she never married. Her ministers hoped she would give birth to an heir, and many important men, including Philip II of Spain, hoped to win power by marrying her. But Elizabeth didn't want to share her position. Instead she told people that she was "married to England".

The thick, white make-up Elizabeth wore when she was older contained lead, which eventually destroyed her skin.

Wealthy women copied her dresses, which had large ruff collars and were embroidered with jewels.

This portrait was painted when Elizabeth was about 55.

All change

Elizabeth made England Protestant again. She wanted everyone to go to the same kind of church, which became known as the Anglican Church. But, unlike her predecessors, she didn't make life difficult for people with other beliefs - unless they actually plotted against her.

Great entertainment

Art and culture flourished at Elizabeth's court under the influence of the Renaissance. The queen encouraged artists such as Nicholas Hilliard, and musicians such as Thomas Tallis, John Dowland and William Byrd gave concerts in private houses and playhouses.

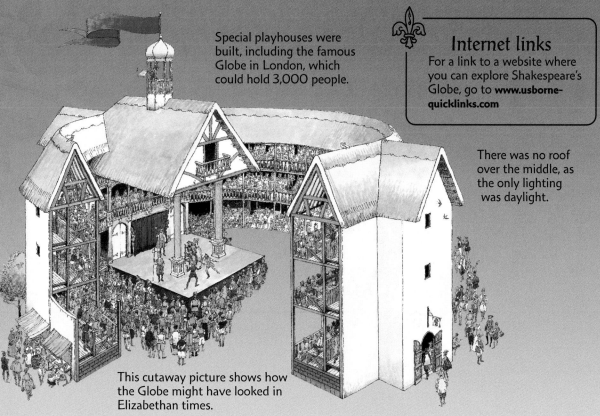

Special playhouses were built, including the famous Globe in London, which could hold 3,000 people.

There was no roof over the middle, as the only lighting was daylight.

This cutaway picture shows how the Globe might have looked in Elizabethan times.

Internet links

For a link to a website where you can explore Shakespeare's Globe, go to **www.usborne-quicklinks.com**

Rich and poor

The rich prospered during Elizabeth's reign, and spent their money on grand houses, furniture and clothes. But some ordinary people were still very poor. A new law was made to make sure all districts provided work for the poor and shelter for those who couldn't work.

A Tudor celebrity

William Shakespeare was one of the most famous writers of all time and a star of the Elizabethan stage. He wrote at least 36 plays, including *Romeo and Juliet*, *Macbeth* and *Hamlet*. Other great writers of the period include Christopher Marlowe, Edmund Spenser, John Donne and Ben Jonson.

Did you know? Many English words and phrases, such as 'leapfrog', 'lonely' and 'countless', were originally invented by Shakespeare.

Exploring the world

The Tudor period was a great age of exploration. Spanish and Portuguese seafarers brought back silver from South America and discovered sea routes to the East Indies, also known as the Spice Islands. This was a major discovery, as they could now bring back valuable silks and spices from India and China much cheaper than by land. Elizabeth encouraged her sailors to search for new lands and treasures too.

A great adventurer

The first English sea captain to sail all the way around the world was Francis Drake, who set sail across the Atlantic in 1577. Some of his ships were lost in stormy seas, but he continued on into the Pacific, then to the Spice Islands and Africa, before returning home with silver, gold and pearls he had looted from Spanish ships.

This 19th century painting shows Elizabeth knighting Drake on board his ship, the *Golden Hind*.

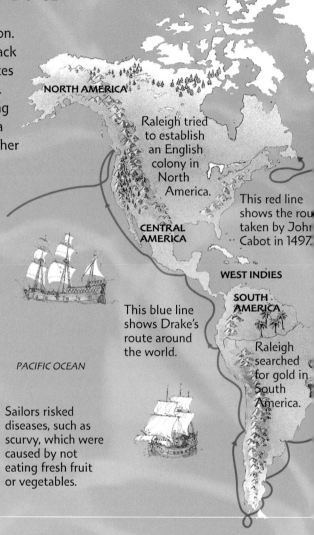

NORTH AMERICA

Raleigh tried to establish an English colony in North America.

This red line shows the rou taken by John Cabot in 1497.

CENTRAL AMERICA

WEST INDIES

SOUTH AMERICA

This blue line shows Drake's route around the world.

Raleigh searched for gold in South America.

PACIFIC OCEAN

Sailors risked diseases, such as scurvy, which were caused by not eating fresh fruit or vegetables.

The search for gold

Sir Walter Raleigh was one of Elizabeth's most popular courtiers. He attempted to establish a colony in North America, named Virginia, after Elizabeth, the 'Virgin Queen'. Raleigh also led expeditions to South America, hoping for gold. He didn't find any, but he brought back food, such as potatoes, that had never been seen before in England.

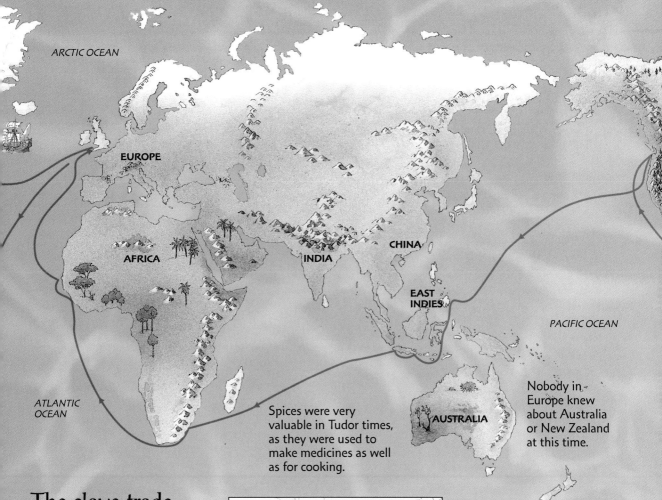

ARCTIC OCEAN

EUROPE

AFRICA

INDIA

CHINA

EAST
INDIES

PACIFIC OCEAN

ATLANTIC
OCEAN

Spices were very
valuable in Tudor times,
as they were used to
make medicines as well
as for cooking.

AUSTRALIA

Nobody in
Europe knew
about Australia
or New Zealand
at this time.

The slave trade

Sir John Hawkins, an
Elizabethan sea captain,
established a route between
Africa and the New World.
By the 17th century, this was
used as a trade triangle (see
map). African slaves were
taken to the New World to
work on cotton and sugar
plantations. The cotton and
sugar were shipped back to
the British Isles.

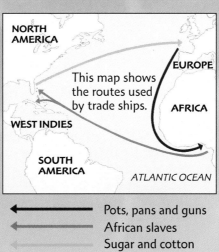

NORTH
AMERICA

EUROPE

This map shows
the routes used
by trade ships.

AFRICA

WEST INDIES

SOUTH
AMERICA

ATLANTIC OCEAN

← Pots, pans and guns
← African slaves
← Sugar and cotton

Stolen treasure

Elizabeth gave her sailors
permission to attack
Spanish treasure ships
coming from the New
World, but this made
England very unpopular
with Spanish seafarers.
Drake was so feared by
the Spaniards that they
nicknamed him 'the
Dragon'.

Did you know? Sir John Hawkins introduced tobacco to England from the New World.
At first, people thought it was a good cure for coughs!

19

Plots and spies

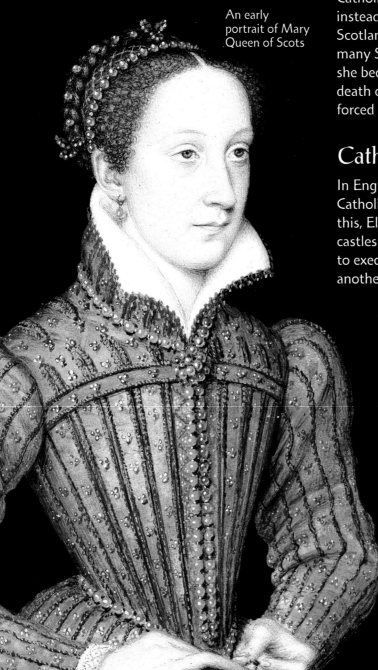

An early portrait of Mary Queen of Scots

Despite Elizabeth's popularity with her subjects, the country was still a hotbed of plots and counter-plots, as some Catholics attempted to make England Catholic again.

Mary Queen of Scots

As Elizabeth had no children, her Catholic cousin, Mary Stuart, queen of Scotland, was next in line for the throne. Some English Catholics even thought she should be queen instead of Elizabeth. But she was unpopular in Scotland. Having spent her early life in France, many Scots considered her a foreigner. When she became involved in a scandal over the death of her husband, Lord Darnley, she was forced to abdicate and flee to England.

Catholic plots

In England, though, Mary became the focus of Catholic plots to replace the queen. To prevent this, Elizabeth kept her prisoner in various castles for 19 years. Her ministers advised her to execute Mary, but she was reluctant to kill another queen, especially her own cousin.

Walsingham's spies

One of Elizabeth's ministers, Sir Francis Walsingham, ran a network of spies specially to uncover plots. One spy found a letter written in code from Mary, in which she agreed to have Elizabeth killed. This evidence finally convinced Elizabeth to have Mary executed.

Internet links

For a link to a website where you can play a spy game and try to crack Mary's secret code, go to **www.usborne-quicklinks.com**

Spanish spies

After Mary's execution, Philip II of Spain grew even more determined to make England Catholic, so he decided to invade. He had become increasingly angry about English raids on Spanish ships in the Caribbean - especially as his spies discovered Elizabeth was taking a share of the treasure herself. To add to his fury, she was also helping Protestants rebel against their Spanish rulers in the Netherlands.

The Armada

English spies found Philip was sending a fleet of ships, called an Armada, to England. In 1588, warned in advance, English sailors harrassed the Armada as it sailed up the Channel. They deliberately set fire to eight of their own ships and sent them crashing into the Spanish ones, driving them out of the port of Calais.

Defeat and retreat

The next morning, the Armada was defeated at the Battle of Gravelines, near Calais. The Spaniards sailed north, hoping to attack again. But storms wrecked many of their ships and the rest sailed around Scotland and Ireland back to Spain. Crowds cheered, as Elizabeth gave a speech in London thanking God for victory over Spain. Many Protestants saw their success as a sign that God was on their side.

The red lines show the route of the Armada.

ENGLAND
Battle of Gravelines
Calais
FRANCE
SPAIN

The Spanish had more ships and men, but English ships were faster and easier to turn.

Did you know? In 1587, Sir Francis Drake destroyed part of the Armada at the port of Cadiz in Spain. The incident was known as 'singeing the King of Spain's beard'.

Life in Tudor towns

In Tudor times, the population was rising and fewer people were needed to work in the countryside, so they flocked to the towns for work. Towns expanded rapidly, becoming dirty and overcrowded. Some people found work, but others were forced to beg or steal.

Finding work

Tudor towns were hubs of activity, with new industries, such as glass and paper making and book printing, providing some people with work. Merchants sold all kind of goods such as wool and iron. Each town had an open-air market, where farmers brought their produce to sell. Goods from overseas, such as sugar, cotton and tobacco, were brought by ship to London, Bristol and other ports.

Education

Most boys learned a trade or craft and girls learned to cook and sew. Only a few children were taught to read and write - usually by a local teacher, using chalk on a piece of slate. Pencils were not invented until the 1560s, and even then they were very expensive. Boys from wealthy families were taught Latin and law by tutors who came to their houses. A few of them went to the new grammar schools that were set up for the first time.

Internet links

For a link to a website where you can find out all kinds of fascinating facts about Tudor life, go to **www.usborne-quicklinks.com**

Food and drink

Most people had a very basic diet: bread, cheese, vegetables and fish, with a little meat. Only the wealthy could afford luxuries like sugar. They also ate exotic birds, such as swans, herons and peacocks. Everyone was dependent on the harvest. So, if it was bad, people could starve to death. There were two terrible famines in Tudor times.

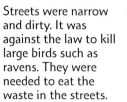

This picture shows a typical street in a Tudor town.

This farmer has come to town to sell bales of wool.

Streets were narrow and dirty. It was against the law to kill large birds such as ravens. They were needed to eat the waste in the streets.

Sewage and waste were poured into open drains.

A raven

A parish church

Most buildings had tiled roofs and were made of wooden frames filled with plaster.

Men being held in a pillory.

An inn

A pickpocket

Market stalls

The market place

Craftsmen and storekeepers hung painted signs from their buildings.

Crime and punishment

There was no police force, but strict laws were enforced by local officers known as constables and Justices of the Peace, and punishments were harsh. Anyone found begging without permission was flogged. Dishonest people were locked in a wooden frame, known as a pillory, where people could throw things at them. Murderers and thieves were hanged. Nobles accused of treason were beheaded, and people who spoke against the Church could be burned.

Did you know? The first London street map was made in 1559.

23

A Stuart king

The Tudor dynasty came to end in 1603, when Elizabeth died after a long and glorious reign. Her heir was James VI of Scotland, the son of Mary Queen of Scots. As James I, he became the first Stuart king of England, and the first king to rule Scotland as well as England, Ireland and Wales.

Differences of opinion

The English welcomed James, but his policies soon made him unpopular. He believed strongly in something called 'Divine Right', which meant that a king's power came from God and nobody had the right to question his decisions. This offended some members of Parliament who were starting to want more power in government themselves. James was Anglican and wanted everyone to be Anglican too. But there were Catholics and extreme Protestants, known as Puritans, who were disappointed that James was not more tolerant of their beliefs.

A portrait of James I, the first Stuart to rule England

The Gunpowder Plot

In 1605, a group of discontented Catholics plotted to blow up the Houses of Parliament, with the king inside. One plotter, Guy Fawkes, was actually caught in the act, with barrels of gunpowder. The plotters were all hung, drawn and quartered - a particularly horrible death. Models of Guy Fawkes are still burned every year on November 5th, in memory of the plot.

Internet links

For a link to a website where you can play a game and try to stop Guy Fawkes from blowing up the Houses of Parliament, go to **www.usborne-quicklinks.com**

An old print showing eight plotters conspiring together to blow up Parliament

This cutaway picture of the *Mayflower* shows what life might have been like on board.

Sailors are taking down the sails to prepare for a storm ahead.

People cooked and slept below the deck. Food was stored in barrels.

The *Mayflower's* voyage across the Atlantic took 66 days. One person died and one was born on board.

Pilgrims

In 1620, a group of 102 Puritans, known as the 'Pilgrims', set sail in the *Mayflower* for a new life in North America. They were attracted by the chance to worship as they wanted, as well as the prospect of land. The area they settled in became known as New England. Life was hard, but they established a colony and exported new foods back to England, such as turkeys and corn.

Pomp and majesty

James loved showing off his royal power. He appointed an architect named Inigo Jones to design the splendid Banqueting House in London, where masques (elaborate plays including opera and dance) were held. The king commissioned the playwright Ben Johnson to write some for him, and some were designed especially to glorify James's reign.

Court and Parliament

The king annoyed Parliament by asking for money to pay for his unpopular policies. He grew fond of certain courtiers, especially one named George Villiers, and spent lots of money on them. Villiers was given the title Duke of Buckingham, but he was unpopular with Parliament and made bad political decisions. When he tried to arrange a marriage between James's son, Charles, and a Spanish princess, the princess refused.

Did you know? James I commissioned the King James Bible, which is still used in many churches today. He also wrote books condemning tobacco and witchcraft.

Charles I

Charles I, James's son, had even more disagreements with Parliament about religion and money than his father. Although he was an Anglican, Parliament feared that Charles really wanted to make England Catholic again. He chose a French Catholic princess, Henrietta Maria, as his wife, and William Laud, the man he appointed as Archbishop of Canterbury, put back most of the statues and paintings in churches that Protestants had removed. Eventually the rift between the king and Parliament grew so bad it led to a bitter civil war, which split the country in two.

A portrait of Henrietta Maria by the Flemish artist, Anthony van Dyck

Art lover

Charles built up an outstanding art collection. He invited the Flemish artist, Peter Paul Rubens, to paint the magnificent ceiling in the Banqueting House in memory of James I, and commissioned many portraits by another Flemish artist, Anthony van Dyck. He was so impressed with van Dyck's work, that he knighted him.

This portrait by van Dyck shows Charles I elegantly dressed. Many MPs disapproved of his extravagance, which put the country further into debt.

Eleven years' tyranny

Eventually Charles found Parliament so hard to deal with that, for 11 years, he tried to rule the country and to raise money without it. Some people called this period the 'eleven years' tyranny'.

Revolts and massacres

Charles faced problems both in Ireland and Scotland. He appointed the Earl of Strafford to rule Ireland for him. Some Irish Catholics felt threatened by the number of English and Scottish Protestants settling there. Later, they revolted and massacred 3,000 Protestants. In Scotland, Laud tried to introduce his version of Protestantism, but most Scots refused to accept it, as they were Presbyterian, which was closer to Puritanism. Riots broke out. Thousands signed a Covenant attacking the changes.

The Long Parliament

In 1640, Charles was forced to recall Parliament to ask for money to deal with the Scots. This Parliament remained in session until 1660. A group of MPs, led by John Pym, introduced laws to try to limit the king's power. One law required him to call Parliament every three years.

Internet links

For a link to a website where you can play the part of Charles I and see if you can avoid civil war, go to **www.usborne-quicklinks.com**

Civil war breaks out

Charles was furious at the attempts to limit his powers. In January, 1642, he burst into the House of Commons and demanded the arrest of the five leading MPs who had opposed him, including Pym. But they had been warned in advance and had already escaped. Charles left London, raised an army of Royalist supporters and declared war. His opponents, the Parliamentarians, gathered supporters to fight against him. By October 1642, fighting had broken out.

This map shows which areas mainly supported Parliament, and which supported the king, at the outbreak of war in 1642.

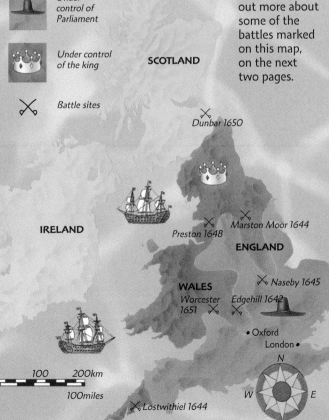

Under control of Parliament

Under control of the king

SCOTLAND

Battle sites

You can find out more about some of the battles marked on this map, on the next two pages.

Dunbar 1650

IRELAND

Preston 1648

Marston Moor 1644

ENGLAND

Naseby 1645

WALES

Worcester 1651

Edgehill 1642

• Oxford

London •

0   100   200km

0   100miles

Lostwithiel 1644

N
W   E
S

 Did you know? In 1635, Charles introduced the first public postal service to Britain. It took ten days to send a letter from London to Edinburgh.

27

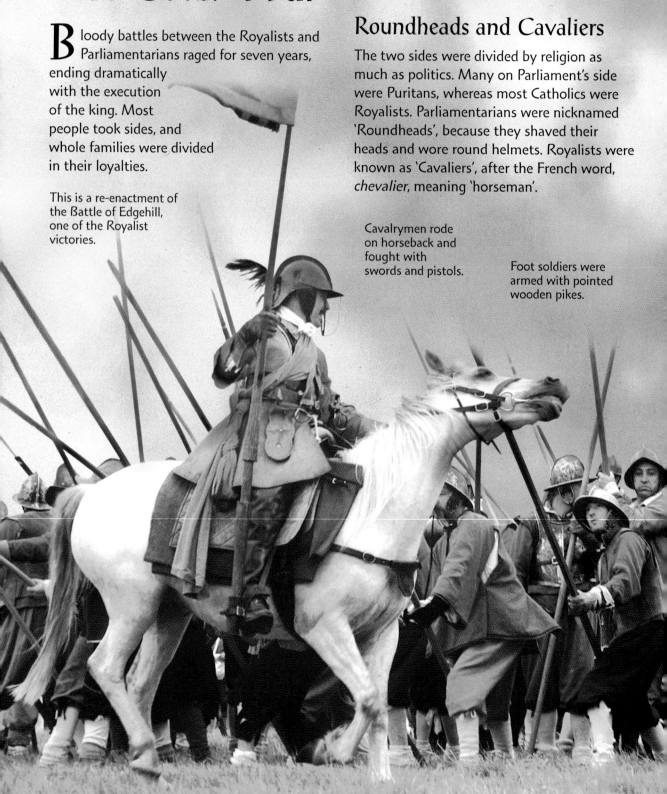

The Civil War

Bloody battles between the Royalists and Parliamentarians raged for seven years, ending dramatically with the execution of the king. Most people took sides, and whole families were divided in their loyalties.

This is a re-enactment of the Battle of Edgehill, one of the Royalist victories.

Roundheads and Cavaliers

The two sides were divided by religion as much as politics. Many on Parliament's side were Puritans, whereas most Catholics were Royalists. Parliamentarians were nicknamed 'Roundheads', because they shaved their heads and wore round helmets. Royalists were known as 'Cavaliers', after the French word, *chevalier*, meaning 'horseman'.

Cavalrymen rode on horseback and fought with swords and pistols.

Foot soldiers were armed with pointed wooden pikes.

The first battles

Charles made Oxford his base, gathered support for his army and set off for London. Helped by Charles's nephew, Prince Rupert of the Rhine, they made advances at the Battle of Edgehill. But the Roundheads stopped them from reaching the city. In 1644, the Scots joined forces with the Roundheads, and beat the Cavaliers at Marston Moor. Now the Roundheads controlled the North of England.

Musketeers used guns, called muskets, which were accurate, but heavy to carry.

The New Model Army

Until the Civil War, armies had been made up of local troops raised by nobles and councils. But in 1645 a Roundhead officer named Oliver Cromwell decided to reorganize the army, for the first time employing full-time, paid and trained men. Cromwell's New Model Army went on to crush the Cavaliers at Naseby. After more defeats, Charles gave himself up to the Scots, who handed him over to Parliament. He was imprisoned, but managed to escape.

The Scots change sides

In 1648, the Scots changed sides to support Charles. But later that year the Roundheads decisively defeated Royalist forces at Preston. The leaders of the New Model Army saw Charles's alliance with Scotland as treason and argued that he should be put on trial.

The king's trial

Charles argued that the courts had no authority to try him, but the army surrounded the House of Commons, trying to keep out any MPs who would vote against putting the king on trial. This Parliament was known as the 'Rump'. The extremists, led by Cromwell, had already decided the verdict: Charles was sentenced to death and the monarchy abolished. On a freezing cold January day in 1649, the king was beheaded outside the Banqueting House in London. Proud till the end, Charles asked for an extra shirt to wear, so the crowd wouldn't think he was shivering with fear.

Did you know? Prince Rupert had a white dog, named Boy, which followed him into battle and became his mascot.

The Commonwealth

The execution of the king amounted almost to a revolution. For the first time in a thousand years, the country had no king or queen. Instead, it was ruled by Parliament, led by Oliver Cromwell, who was now the most powerful man in the land. This period, which lasted eleven years, is known as the Commonwealth.

Unlike kings, Oliver Cromwell preferred not to be flattered in paintings. This portrait shows him with a red face and shiny nose.

Rebellions and invasions

Cromwell was determined to punish the Irish Catholics, who were now rebelling in support of Charles I's son, Charles Stuart. So Cromwell took his army to Ireland, where they fought off the rebels, killing thousands of them. Meanwhile, Charles was crowned king of Scotland and led an army to invade England. Cromwell defeated him at the Battle of Worcester, but Charles escaped. He had many adventures, including hiding from Cromwell's army in an oak tree, before fleeing to live in exile in France.

An engraving showing Charles hiding in the oak tree

Lord Protector

In 1653, Cromwell took the title of Lord Protector and ruled with a succession of Parliaments, searching for a system of government that worked. But he argued with each one and dismissed them all. Finally, he ruled without Parliament, a bit like a dictator, just as Charles I had done. When Cromwell died in 1658, his son Richard became Lord Protector. But he had nothing like his father's character and couldn't control the Parliament or the army. So the army invited back the surviving members of the 'Rump Parliament'.

 Did you know? In the reign of the next king, Charles II, Parliament ordered Oliver Cromwell's dead body to be put on trial for treason. It was found guilty and hanged.

Simple life

Cromwell's Puritan supporters expected everyone to work hard and live a very simple life. Churches were stripped of all decoration - paintings, statues and stained glass windows - and inns and playhouses were closed. Traditions, such as bear-baiting and maypole dancing were forbidden, and even Christmas and Easter celebrations were banned and turned into days of fasting instead. Soldiers went to people's houses and took away their Christmas dinner. Many complained that Cromwell was using the army to impose his views.

A woman in simple Puritan dress

Sugar and slaves

During this period, the trade in sugar and slaves between Europe, Africa and the West Indies was growing, and Cromwell hoped England could profit from it. In 1651, he sent troops to establish trading rights with the island of Barbados, where English settlers had already set up thriving sugar plantations. Then, in 1655, English troops seized Jamaica from Spanish colonists and plantations were set up there too.

Trade rivalry

In the early 17th century, the Dutch were the most successful trading nation in Europe. But the English came to rival them, after expanding their colonies overseas and improving their navy. In 1652, the first trade war broke out between the two countries, over who was to control trading routes. The Dutch were defeated and forced to limit their trade with English colonies. Further wars followed, and by the 1680s, the English emerged as the most powerful trading nation in Europe.

This painting shows a battle in the second Anglo-Dutch trade war, which was fought entirely in the North Sea.

The Merry Monarch

An army officer named General Monck invited Charles I's son back from exile to become King Charles II. Charles was a cultured and fun-loving man, who encouraged art, science, drama and music. After years of dull Puritan rule, his subjects welcomed him, nicknaming him 'the Merry Monarch'. He married a Portuguese princess, Catherine of Braganza. They didn't have any children together, but Charles had 14 illegitimate children with his many mistresses.

This portrait shows Charles wearing a long, curly wig - a popular fashion at the court of Louis XIV of France.

A portrait of Nell Gwyn

Nell Gwyn

Playhouses were opened again, to the delight of the public, and women were allowed to act on stage for the first time. One popular actress, Nell Gwyn, started life as an orange seller in a playhouse the king attended. He was attracted by her good looks and wit, and she became one of his best-loved mistresses.

King and Parliament

The monarchy was popular again and relations between the king and Parliament began well. The new king called Parliament frequently and took its advice, as he had no intention of risking another civil war. Parliament didn't punish Charles for his extravagant lifestyle or for the periods when he ruled alone.

A secret deal

But in 1670, Charles negotiated a secret deal with Louis XIV of France: he promised to become a Catholic and to continue fighting with the French against the Dutch, in exchange for £200,000 a year. This was a dangerous move, as people were already suspicious that he had Catholic sympathies. When they discovered James, his brother and heir, had become a Catholic, they were even more worried. Some MPs even tried to prevent James from ever becoming king.

Crown Jewels

In 1671, an Irish adventurer named Colonel Blood was caught attempting to steal the Crown Jewels from the Jewel House at the Tower of London. Charles was amused by the Colonel's stories and sense of adventure. So, instead of punishing him, he awarded him with a pension and some land.

The first political parties

During Charles II's reign, two organized political parties emerged. MPs who wanted to exclude James from the succession became known as Whigs. Those who wanted James to be king were called Tories. Both parties argued their case in printed pamphlets.

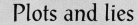

An engraving of Titus Oates in a pillory

Plots and lies

In 1678, a Protestant named Titus Oates spread talk of a Catholic plot to kill Charles and make James king. It became known as the 'Popish Plot'. Panic spread and the army arrested over 2,000 Catholics - before it was discovered Oates had invented the plot himself.

In 1683, some Whigs plotted to kill Charles and James and declare Charles's eldest illegitimate son, the Protestant Duke of Monmouth, king instead. The plot failed and the plotters were executed. When Charles died in 1685, the Whigs were so discredited that the Tories took control of Parliament, and James became king with little opposition. Although Charles had lived as a Protestant, on his deathbed, he confessed to his Catholic beliefs.

Coffee was first introduced to Britain from Arabia in the early 1600s. Coffee houses became popular meeting places, especially for plotters.

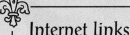

Internet links

For a link to a website where you can find out about the history of coffee, go to **www. usborne-quicklinks.com**

Did you know? In 1664, British troops seized the Dutch town of New Amsterdam in America. It was renamed New York, after Charles's brother, James, Duke of York.

33

Plague and fire

Early in Charles II's reign, a terrible and fatal disease, known as bubonic plague, attacked London, killing thousands of people. In Stuart times, the city was overcrowded and filthy. Waste was thrown straight into the streets and people didn't wash much. The germs that brought the plague were carried by fleas living in the fur of black rats. The summer of 1665 was hotter than usual, providing ideal conditions for the rats and their fleas to breed.

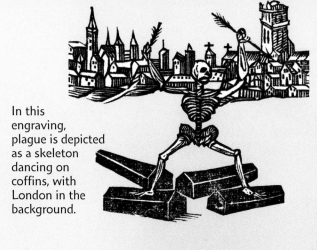

In this engraving, plague is depicted as a skeleton dancing on coffins, with London in the background.

The victims

One of the first signs that you had the plague was the appearance of black lumps appearing on your body. Some people died after only a few hours, but others suffered for days. The only way to stop the plague from spreading was to deal with it ruthlessly. Victims and their families were sealed inside their houses and left to die. A red cross was painted on the doors to warn passers-by.

Great escape

Anyone who could afford to - merchants, lawyers, clergy and even surgeons - left the city. Nobles fled to their country estates and the king moved his court to Salisbury, and then to Oxford. Businesses closed and soon the streets were deserted. But some people carried the germs with them to the country and the plague soon spread.

Desperate measures

Nobody knew how to cure the plague. Some thought it was caused by poisonous gases in the air, and they lit fires to try to drive it away. Others thought God had sent the plague to punish people for their sins. Some fasted or prayed and others made magic potions. Eventually, what helped kill it off was the arrival of cold winter weather.

Doctors wore leather robes with hoods and gloves. Their masks had glass eyeholes and beaks stuffed with herbs, which were supposed to ward away sickness.

The Great Fire

The following summer was also very hot, and a great fire swept through London, destroying most of the city. The fire started in a bakery, and strong winds helped it spread rapidly through the tightly-packed wooden houses. Within hours, whole streets were ablaze. It raged for four days until the wind died down. But, by this time, four-fifths of London was destroyed, and over 100,000 people had become homeless. Amazingly, only nine people died.

Fighting the fire

There was no fire service in those days and only a few houses had supplies of water. So people tried to stop the fire from spreading by blowing up or pulling down buildings in the path of the flames. Everyone took part, even the king.

Charles II ordered buildings to be pulled down to stop the fire from spreading to the Tower of London, where gunpowder was stored.

Internet links

For a link to a website where you see pictures of London before and after the Great Fire, go to **www.usborne-quicklinks.com**

Old St. Paul's Cathedral and hundreds of churches were destroyed in the fire.

People tried to flee the fire by crossing to the south side of the River Thames to safety.

 Did you know? The fire started in Pudding Lane and ended at Pie Corner.

Life in Stuart times

After the Great Fire, Charles II ordered London to be rebuilt in brick and stone instead of wood, to prevent another catastrophic fire. He commissioned the architect, Sir Christopher Wren, to design a new St. Paul's Cathedral, as well as over 50 smaller churches throughout the city. Wide, paved avenues and tree-lined squares replaced the old narrow, winding streets. Although most people still lived in poverty, quality of life improved for those who could afford it.

This portrait of Sir Christopher Wren shows St. Paul's Cathedral in the background. The arches and domes are in the Baroque style, influenced by Italian Renaissance architects.

Home improvements

For the first time, many houses were designed with separate rooms for living, eating and sleeping in. Furniture was more elaborately carved and chairs were more comfortable. Some were even upholstered with leather and horsehair.

This carved chair was made to commemorate Charles II's reign.

Pirates

The 17th century was an age of piracy on the high seas. Traders and explorers on long sea journeys risked being attacked by pirates, looking for ships to plunder. One notorious pirate, Henry Morgan, built his reputation by leading daring attacks on Spanish ships in the West Indies. Charles II made him governor of Jamaica in return for defending the island.

The business world

There were many changes in the Stuart period which made business easier. Banknotes, cheques, printed labels, envelopes, insurance and newspapers were all introduced for the first time. Increased trade and expensive wars meant the government needed more money. The Bank of England was founded in 1694 by a trader named William Paterson to lend the government money.

 Did you know? Charles II's patronage helped to make the races at Newmarket popular. Ever since, racing has been known as the 'sport of kings'.

A cultured life

Music, literature and drama all flourished in Stuart times. Henry Purcell, one of England's most famous composers, wrote many pieces including the opera *Dido and Aeneas*. Great works of literature included John Milton's *Paradise Lost*, John Bunyan's *Pilgrim's Progress* and John Dryden's poetry and plays. Great adventurers and explorers inspired novels such as *Robinson Crusoe* by Daniel Defoe and *Gulliver's Travels* by Jonathan Swift. Samuel Pepys and John Evelyn wrote famous diaries, which have helped historians learn more about what daily life was like.

This early engraving shows two witches and a black dog, thought to be a witch's helper.

Internet links

For a link to a website where you can read extracts from Samuel Pepys's diaries, go to
www.usborne-quicklinks.com

The weather was different in Stuart times. The Thames used to flow more slowly and sometimes even froze. Frost fairs were held on the ice, where people could enjoy entertainment such as puppet shows, ice-skating and bear-baiting.

Witches and witchcraft

In Stuart times many people still believed in witches, although this declined as scientific knowledge increased. Witch hunts reached a peak in the 1640s, when a lawyer named Matthew Hopkins tracked down and sentenced 230 people to death for witchcraft. The accused person was tested by being thrown into water. If they drowned, they were judged innocent. If they lived, they were found guilty and executed. In 1647, Hopkins took his own test and was found guilty and executed.

This painting shows the longest frost fair in the history of London, from December 1683 to February 1684.

Scientific discoveries

The Stuart period was a time of great scientific activity. Many earlier scientific ideas had been based on a mixture of religion, superstition and guesswork. But the influence of the Renaissance made people question the world around them, and scientists began doing experiments to test their ideas.

The Royal Society

In the 1640s, a group of intellectuals, including Sir Christopher Wren and Samuel Pepys, began meeting reguarly to discuss ideas and carry out scientific experiments. In 1662, Charles II gave the group a charter and it was named the Royal Society. The king even helped with some of the experiments.

One member, Robert Boyle, invented the air pump. Another, Robert Hooke, developed a microscope. This meant that, for the first time, people could observe animals that were too small to see with the human eye alone.

This drawing of a flea was made after looking at it through Hooke's microscope.

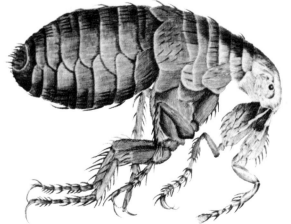

A true genius

Sir Isaac Newton was one of the greatest scientists of all time. He originated the idea that science and mathematics could explain every problem. He was the first person to realize that a force, which we call gravity, pulls objects to the ground, and concluded that gravity is what keeps the moon in orbit around the Earth. Newton made important discoveries about light, and invented the mirror telescope, which enabled astronomers to study the stars. He was the first man to be knighted for his scientific work.

Sir Isaac Newton became President of the Royal Society in 1703.

Sun, moon and stars

In 1675, Charles II set up the Royal Observatory in Greenwich, near London, where astronomers could study the sun, moon and stars. This helped them to work out the date, tell the time and navigate at sea.

The telescope used by Sir Isaac Newton to study the stars

Halley's comet

In 1682, a brilliant astronomer named Edmund Halley, predicted the return of a comet that he saw. The same comet had also been seen in 1066, 1531 and 1607. When it reappeared in 1758, 16 years after his death, the comet was named after him.

Halley's comet appeared in 1066, at the Battle of Hastings, and was depicted in the Bayeux Tapestry, shown here.

Medicine

Until the 17th century, little was known about how the body worked or what caused disease. Only one in ten people was expected to reach the age of 40. Operations were done by barber surgeons, who set broken bones, as well as shaving people and cutting hair. They also bled people as this was thought to cure them. In the early 17th century, the Church finally allowed doctors to cut up bodies to study how they work. This made further discoveries possible. In 1628, a physician named William Harvey discovered the secret of circulation, when he realized the heart was a pump which makes blood flow around the body.

A new age

Here are some of the Stuart inventions which opened the way for a new industrial age:

● In 1626, Francis Bacon discovered that freezing meat would preserve it. He experimented by stuffing a chicken with snow.

● In 1694, Henry Winstanley started building the first lighthouse, to warn ships away from the Eddystone Rock, off the coast of Cornwall.

● In 1701, Jethro Tull invented a seed drill. Before this, seeds were scattered by hand.

● In 1705, Thomas Newcomen invented a steam engine, which was used to pump flood water from coal mines.

● In 1709, Abraham Darby discovered how to purify coal to make a substance called coke. Coke could be used to work more efficiently with iron and steel.

This painting by the Dutch artist Rembrandt shows a group of 17th century doctors examining the arm of a dead man.

Internet links

For a link to a website where you can listen to actors playing 17th century scientists discussing their ideas, go to **www.usborne-quicklinks.com**

Did you know? Many people were superstitious about illness. Some believed that a disease called scrofula could be cured by touching the monarch's hand.

A Catholic king

James II was in a strong position when he became king, despite being a Catholic. He had a permanent army and a Parliament dominated by loyal Tories. But when he started putting Catholics into positions of power, many Protestants felt threatened. James soon became unpopular and he abdicated after only three years on the throne.

The Monmouth Rebellion

Four months into James's reign, there was a rebellion to overthrow him, led by the Protestant Duke of Monmouth. But James had plenty of support and his army defeated Monmouth at the Battle of Sedgemoor. Trials followed and Monmouth and 300 Protestant rebels were charged with treason and executed, while 800 others were taken to Barbados as slaves. The trials were so harsh, they became known as the 'Bloody Assizes'. Many of the Protestants who had supported James now turned against him.

Religious differences

In 1687, James tried to take the law into his own hands, by issuing an order called the 'Declaration of Indulgence', to abolish the laws against Catholics. But Parliament refused to accept it. When James ordered the Declaration to be read out in every church, seven bishops protested. Many Protestants were angry when James put the bishops on trial. But when his judges found them 'not guilty', it made a fool of the king.

Internet links

For a link to a website where you can find out about James II and his Jacobite heirs, go to **www.usborne-quicklinks.com**

James II, a year after he became king

Did you know? James II and his brother, Charles II, made sailing a popular sport, when they took part in the first yacht race down the River Thames, in 1661.

A Catholic heir

James and his first wife, Anne Hyde, had two daughters, Mary and Anne, who were both Protestants. Many MPs tolerated James's pro-Catholic polices because Princess Mary was the heir and would eventually become queen. But things changed dramatically in 1688, when Mary of Modena, James's Catholic second wife, gave birth to a son named James. Protestants were horrified, as it meant the new heir to the throne was a Catholic. Some even spread the idea that the baby was not really the king's son, but had been smuggled into the queen's bed in a warming pan.

This crown was made specially for Mary of Modena to wear when she and James were crowned in 1685.

The Glorious Revolution

Almost immediately, some MPs asked Princess Mary's Dutch husband, the Protestant Prince William of Orange, to help save England from becoming Catholic. William landed in Torbay, in Devon, with an army of 15,000 men, in an invasion which became known as the 'Glorious Revolution'. A few months later, Parliament declared that James had abdicated and William and Mary were crowned King and Queen.

The king flees

Fearing execution, James escaped down the River Thames in a boat, joining his wife and son in Paris, where they all lived in exile. Some people, known as Jacobites (after the Latin for James), continued to support him, and believed he should be king. When James died in 1701, Louis XIV of France recognized his 12-year-old son as James III of England.

This painting of William of Orange landing at Torbay was painted by a Dutch artist, so the buildings don't look very English.

William and Mary

William and Mary were appointed by Parliament to reign together. This put an end to the idea that kings and queens were appointed by God, and began a new relationship between Parliament and the king. After Mary died in 1694, William ruled alone.

This plate, showing William and Mary's coronation, is in the style of Dutch Delft ware, which was popular during their reign.

More power to Parliament

In 1689, William and Mary agreed to limit the powers of the monarchy, in a 'Bill of Rights' presented to them by Parliament. It stated that all future monarchs had to be Protestant, and that they couldn't keep an army or raise taxes without permission from Parliament, which would have to be called every three years.

Internet links

For a link to a website where you can take a virtual tour of Hampton Court Palace, go to **www.usborne-quicklinks.com**

The Battle of the Boyne

The exiled James II hadn't given up the hope of regaining his throne. In 1689, he landed in Ireland and, with the help of French and Irish Catholics, attempted to take control from the Protestants who had settled there. He held the Protestant town of Derry under siege, but failed to capture it. Finally, William defeated him in 1690, at the Battle of the Boyne, and gave land in Northern Ireland to the Protestants. Derry was renamed Londonderry.

Massacre at Glencoe

Although most Lowland Scots were Presbyterian, many of the Highland clans (families) were Catholic and wanted James II back as king. In 1692, William made them sign an oath of loyalty to him. When the MacDonalds of Glencoe missed the deadline to sign, 38 members of their clan were brutally massacred by their rivals, the Campbells, under orders from the government.

The Grand Alliance

As a Dutchman, King William was concerned about the increasing threat to Dutch independence from the powerful King Louis XIV of France. In 1690, he formed a 'Grand Alliance' between the Netherlands, Austria and England to fight against France. But many English people resented being involved in Dutch problems. The war ended in 1697 with the Treaty of Ryswick, in which France was forced to give up some of its territories.

These tulips were painted by a 17th century artist.

Dutch tulips were so popular that one tulip bulb of a very rare variety could cost as much as a large country house.

Act of Settlement

William and Mary had no children. So in 1701, Parliament passed an 'Act of Settlement', declaring that Mary's sister, Anne, and her heirs, would succeed to the throne. They would be followed by James I's grand-daughter, Sophia, who had married into a German Protestant family, which ruled the state of Hanover. When William died in 1702, Anne became queen.

Sir Christopher Wren designed this grand addition to the royal palace at Hampton Court, near London, during William and Mary's reign.

 Did you know? Even now, some Protestants in Northern Ireland call themselves 'Orangemen', in memory of the support William of Orange gave them.

The last Stuart

Queen Anne, Mary's younger sister, was the last of the Stuart dynasty. She married Prince George of Denmark and had 17 children, but none of them survived. After her death, the crown passed to a German cousin.

Queen Anne wearing a robe edged with ermine

War in Europe

Early in Anne's reign, England became involved in a war in Europe: the War of the Spanish Succession. Charles II of Spain had died in 1700, leaving his vast empire to Prince Philip, grandson of Louis XIV of France. England, Austria and the Netherlands all feared the idea of a union between France and Spain, as it would make France far too powerful. So they formed an alliance, and claimed the throne for Archduke Charles of Austria instead.

The first Churchill

In 1701, war broke out between the two sides. A young general named John Churchill helped win a series of outstanding victories, securing England's reputation as a major European power. He became a national hero. Anne rewarded him with a title, Duke of Marlborough, and a large plot of land, where he built a magnificent palace called Blenheim, named after one of his most famous battles.

Childhood friends

The Queen and the Duke of Marlborough's wife, a courtier named Sarah Churchill, had been close friends since childhood. Sarah's influence helped her husband rise to a position of political influence. But when Sarah tried to persuade Anne to put more Whigs into high office, Anne resisted. Eventually, the two women fell out and the Duke was dismissed from his position in government, despite his popularity and his military success.

A painting of Blenheim Palace in the 1700s

War is over

The Queen then fell under the influence of another courtier, Abigail Masham. Abigail helped her cousin, a Tory named Robert Harley, to become Chancellor of the Exchequer, in charge of finance. Soon Parliament was dominated by Tories, who hoped for peace. In 1713 and 1714, the Treaties of Utrecht were signed, and the war was over at last. A compromise was reached: Prince Philip of France did become king of Spain, but his empire was reduced. Some Spanish territory was given to England, Austria and the Netherlands.

Roads and travel

Travel during this period was still very limited. Poor people either walked and some rode on horseback, but most rarely left the villages where they were born. Wealthy people could afford to take stagecoaches, but they sometimes overturned on badly made roads, or were held up by highwaymen, who demanded passengers' money. Travel slowly began to improve as Turnpike trusts were formed. This meant that anyone who used the roads had to pay for their upkeep.

The United Kingdom

Parliament feared that the Scots might try to make James II's son, James, king of Scotland, because the Scottish Jacobites still didn't accept the 'Act of Settlement'. To prevent this, in 1707, Parliament passed the 'Act of Union'.

The English (middle) and Scottish (bottom) flags were combined to make the Union flag, which became the national flag. The Irish flag was added in 1801.

From now on, England, Scotland, Ireland and Wales were united under one Parliament and the nation became known as the United Kingdom of Great Britain.

The house of Hanover

Anne died in 1714, without any children to succeed her. The throne then passed to the next in line: George, the son of Sophia of Hanover, in Germany, who became George I. Queen Elizabeth II is his direct descendant.

This woodcut shows the London to Henley stagecoach in 1717.

A new era begins

Huge changes had taken place between the reign of Henry Tudor and the death of Queen Anne. Now that England, Ireland, Scotland and Wales were united, a new nation had been formed. Most people were now Protestant, instead of Catholic, but religion was no longer a major cause of quarrels and wars, burning and persecution. The country that the Hanoverians inherited was one of the most powerful in the world, with London at the heart of its trade, industry and culture.

King and Parliament

Parliament's victory in the Civil War, and the 'Bill of Rights' in 1689, meant that kings would never again be as powerful as they had been. The emergence of political parties in Charles II's reign laid the foundations for the two-party system of government which became a model for other countries too. The house of Hanover survived, although the Jacobites continued to try to overthrow them well into the 18th century.

This painting shows English East India Company ships at the British trading post of Bombay, India.

Industry and agriculture

The discoveries and inventions of the Tudor and Stuart period gradually transformed people's lives. Advances in medicine increased life expectancy. New machinery and improvements in the way people worked would lead to an Industrial Revolution over the next hundred years or so. Towns and cities grew, as people flocked to them, attracted by the prospect of work in trade and new industries. In the countryside, new machinery and new farming techniques brought changes which led to an Agricultural Revolution as well.

The start of an empire

Thriving colonies had been established in America, and trading posts and naval bases set up along the coasts of Asia and Africa. Trading companies were formed, bringing back goods such as sugar, tobacco, cotton, dyes and spices, as well as much wealth. Britain was ready to expand its influence overseas and would eventually acquire the largest empire in the history of the world.

Acknowledgements

Every effort has been made to trace the copyright holders of material in this book. If any rights have been omitted, the publishers offer their sincere apologies and will rectify this in any subsequent editions, following notification. The publishers are grateful to the following individuals and organizations for their permission to reproduce material on the following pages (*t = top, m = middle, b = bottom, l = left, r = right*);

Cover © AKG London. **p1** © National Portrait Gallery, London, UK/Bridgeman Art Library. **endpapers, p2-3, 4-5, 6-7, 8-9, 12-13, 16-17** © The Art Archive/ Victoria and Albert Museum London/Sally Chappell. **p3** © Robert Estall/CORBIS. **p4** © The Stapleton Collection/Bridgeman Art Library. **p5** (t) © Society of Antiquaries, London. **p6** © Stapleton Collection/ CORBIS. **p7** (t) By kind permission of the Dean and Chapter of York. **p8** © AKG London. **p9** (t) © The Art Archive/ Musée du Château de Versailles/Dagli Orti; (b) © Hever Castle Ltd. **p10-11** © Patrick Ward/CORBIS. **p9** (t) © Bettmann/ CORBIS. **p12** (t) © The British Library; (b) © The Art Archive/National Gallery of Art Washington/Album/Joseph Martin. **p13** © National Gallery Collection; By kind permission of the Trustees of the National Gallery, London/CORBIS. **p14** (l) © Archivo Iconografico, S.A./CORBIS; (r) © Society of Antiquaries, London. **p15** (r) © The British Library. **p16** © AKG London. **p18** © Mary Evans Picture Library. **p20** The Royal Collection © 2003, Her Majesty Queen Elizabeth II. **p24-25, 26-27, 30-31, 32-33, 34-35, 40-41** © Owen Franken/CORBIS. **p24** (t) © Christie's Images/CORBIS; (b) © Mary Evans Picture Library. **p26** (l) © Arte & Immagini srl/CORBIS; (r) © Lauros/Giraudon/Bridgeman Art Library. **p28-29** © Nigel Hillyard/Sealed Knot; Digital Vision. **p30** (l) © The Art Archive/Pitti Palace, Florence; (r) © Mary Evans Picture Library. **p31** (t) © Rafael Valls Gallery, London, UK/Bridgeman Art Library; (b) © National Maritime Musuem, London. **p32** (l) © The Art Archive/Christ's Hospital/Eileen Tweedy; (t) © The Art Archive/Army and Navy Club/Eileen Tweedy. **p33** (t) © CORBIS; (b) © The Art Archive/British Museum/Eileen Tweedy. **p34** (t) © Plague Skeleton from Decker's a Rod for Runnaways Mal. 601 (1); (b) © Bettman/ CORBIS. **p36** (t) © By kind permission of the Trustees of the Chequers Estate/Bridgeman Art Library; (b) © Private Collection/Bridgeman Art Library. **p37** (t) © Mary Evans Picture Library; (b) © The Art Archive/London Musuem/Eileen Tweedy. **p38-39** © CORBIS. **p38** (t) © Academie des Sciences, Paris, France/Bridgeman Art Library/Lauros/Giraudon/Bridgeman Art Library; (bl) © Mary Evans Picture Library; (br) © The Art Archive/British Museum/Eileen Tweedy. **p39** (b) © Bettmann/CORBIS. **p40** © National Maritime Museum, London. **p41** (t) © Museum of London; (b) The Royal Collection © 2003, Her Majesty Queen Elizabeth II. **p42-43** © Massimo Listri/CORBIS. **p42** (t) © Lambeth Victoria and Albert Museum, London, UK/Bridgeman Art Library. **p43** © Wageningen UR Library. **p44 (t)** © Philip Mould, Historical Portraits Ltd., London, UK/Bridgeman Art Library; (b) © Jarrold Publishing, reproduced by kind permission of the publisher. **p45** (b) © City of Westminster, London, UK/ Bridgeman Art Library. **p46** © British Library, London, UK/Bridgeman Art Library.

Managing designer: Mary Cartwright
Cover design by Neil Francis
Illustrated by David Cuzik, Giacinto Gaudenzi, Jeremy Gower, Inklink Firenze and Janos Marffy
Additional photography by Stef Lumley
Photoshop by Roger Bolton. DTP by Rachel Bright

Index